in the same series

Magic Water
Sam Pig and His Fiddle
The Christmas Box
Sam Pig and the Dragon
Sam Pig and the Wind
Sam Pig and the Hurdy-Gurdy Man
The May Queen

The Adventures of Sam Pig

Sam Pig's Trousers
Alison Uttley

Illustrated by Graham Percy

faber and faber

LONDON · BOSTON

First published in 1940
by Faber and Faber Limited
3 Queen Square London WC1N 3AU
This edition first published in 1989

Printed in Great Britain by
W. S. Cowell Ltd Ipswich

British Library Cataloguing in Publication Data is available

ISBN 0–571–15293–7

Sam Pig's Trousers

Sam Pig was always hard on his trousers. He tore them on the brambles and hooked them in the gorse bushes. He lost little pieces of them in the hawthorns, and he left shreds among the spiky thistles. He rubbed them threadbare with sliding down the rocks of the high pastures, and he wore them into holes when he scrambled through hedges. One always knew where Sam Pig had been by the fragments of checked trousers which clung to thorn and crooked twig. The birds were very glad, and they took bits to make their nests.

The rooks had little snippets like gay pennons dangling from their rookery in the elms, and the chaffinches and yellow-hammers mixed the threads with sheep's wool to line their beds. It seemed as if Sam Pig would provide material for everybody's home in the trees and hedgerows, but trousers won't last for ever, and Sam's were nearly done.

Sister Ann patched the seats and put pieces into the front. She stitched panels in the two

sides, and then she patched and repatched the patches until there was none of the original trousers left. They were a conglomeration of stripes and plaids and spotted scraps, all herring-boned and cross-stitched with green thread.

'Sam's trousers are like a patchwork quilt,' remarked Tom, when Ann held up the queer little garments one evening after she had mended them.

'Pied and speckled like a magpie,' said Bill.

Sam Pig leaned out of the truckle bed where he lay wrapped in a blanket, waiting for Ann to finish the mending. They were the only trousers the little pig possessed, and he had to go to bed early on mending nights.

'I like them patched,' said he indignantly. 'Don't mock at them. I love my old trousers and their nice patches. It's always a suprise when Ann finishes them. Look now! There's a green patch on top of a black patch, on top of a yellow patch, on top of a blue one. And there's lots of pockets

hidden among the patches, spaces where I can keep things. When Ann's stitches burst I stuff things in between.'

'Yes,' frowned Ann. 'I've already taken out a ladybird, and a piece of honeycomb, and some bees and a frog that was leaping up and down, and a stag-beetle that was fighting, not to mention sundry pebbles and oak-apples and snail shells! No wonder you look a clumsy shape with all those things hidden in your patches, Sam! All corners and lumps, you are!'

Sam curled himself under the blanket and laughed till he made the bed shake. She hadn't found the most important thing of all, something that was hidden under the largest patch! If she did – !

Just then Ann gave a shrill cry and dropped the trousers.

'Oh! They've bitten me! Your trousers bit my finger!' she exclaimed, and she put her hand in her mouth and sucked it.

'Trousers can't bite,' said Tom, but Sam dived deeper under the blanket, and laughed all the more.

'What is it, Sam?' asked Tom sternly. 'Confess! What is hidden there in your trousers?'

There was no answer, but from the patch came a pair of ears and two bright eyes. A white mouse poked out its little head. It stared at Ann, it peeped at Sam, and then it bolted down the table leg and into a hole in the floor.

'Now you've lost her! You've lost Jemima!' said Sam crossly, coming up from the blankets. 'She was my pet mouse, and you've lost her. She was a most endearing creature. I kept her in that patch and fed her on crumbs. Is her family safe?'

'Family?' cried Ann, shrilly.

'Family?' echoed Bill and Tom.

'Yes. She has four children. They all live in the patch. They have a nest there. I helped Jemima to make it. I'm the godfather to the children. They know me very well.'

Ann hurriedly unpicked the stitches and brought out a small round nest with four pink mice inside it.

'There they are! Aren't they charming creatures?' cried Sam.

'But they will be lonely without their mother. You must put them by the hole in the floor, Ann, and Jemima will come for them. She'll miss her warm home in my trousers, and the food I gave her.'

Ann carried the nest and placed it close to the hole. In a minute the mother appeared and enticed her brood away.

'Good-bye, Sam,' she squealed in a shrill voice, thin as a grasshopper's chirp. 'Good-bye Sam, and thank you for your hospitality. We are going to travel. It is time my children saw something of the world.'

'Good-bye,' called Sam, leaning out of bed. 'I shall miss you terribly, but we may meet again some day. The world is small.'

'Hm!' sniffed Ann Pig. 'The world may be small, but surely there is room in it for a family of white mice without their coming to live in a patch in your trousers, Sam.'

She threaded her needle and took up a bodkin and cleared away all the odds and ends the mice had left – their pots and frying-pan and toasting fork. She tossed the bits of cheese in the fire and frowned as she brought out a bacon rind.

'Bacon in the house of the four pigs is an insult,' said she sternly.

'It came from the grocer's shop, Ann. Really it did! Jemima's husband brought it for the family,' protested Sam.

'Then it's quite time you had a new pair of trousers, Sam. Jemima's husband bringing bacon rinds! I won't have it! These mice are the last straw!' cried Ann, and she banged the trousers and shook them and threw them back to Sam.

'Yes,' agreed Bill. 'It is time you had new brecks. We can't have a menagerie in our house. You'll keep ants and antelopes hidden in your patches, Sam, if you go on like this.'

'Bears and bisons,' said Tom, shaking his head at Sam.

'Crocodiles and cassowaries,' whispered Sam, quivering with laughter.

'It's no laughing matter. Trousers don't grow on gooseberry bushes.'

'I don't want a new pair,' pouted Sam. 'I know this pair, and they are very comfortable. I know every stitch and cranny, and every ridge and crease and crumple.' He pulled the trousers on and shook himself.

'These will soon be quite worn out. One more tear and they will be done,' said Ann. 'We must get another pair, and where the stuff is to come from in these hard times I don't know. You'd better go collecting, all of you.'

'Collecting what? Trousers? From the scarecrows?' asked Sam.

'No. Sheep's wool. Get it off the hedges and bushes and fences. Everywhere you go you must gather the wool left by the sheep when they scramble through gaps and rub their backs on posts. Then I'll dye the wool and spin it, and make a new pair for you.'

Each day the pigs gathered sheep's wool. They picked it off the wild rose trees, where it was twisted among the thorns. They got it from low

fences under which the sheep had squeezed, and from the rough trunks of hawthorns and oaks where they had rubbed their backs. Sam found a fine bunch of fleecy wool where the flock had pushed under the crooked boughs of an ancient tree to sleep in the hollow beneath. It was surprising what a quantity of wool there was lying about in the country lanes, and each day they brought back their small sacks filled to the brim.

Ann washed the little fleeces and hung them up to dry. The wool was white as snow when she had finished dipping it in the stream. She tied it to a stout stick and swung it in the sunshine till it was dry and light as a feather.

Bill filled a bowl with lichens and mosses and pieces of bark, and Ann dyed the wool.

'What colour will it be?' asked Sam anxiously peering at it. 'I don't want brown or grey or anything dull.'

'It looks like drab,' confessed Ann.

'Oh dear! What a dingy shade!' sighed Sam. 'I don't want miserable gloomy trousers, or I shall be a gloomy little pig.'

'I'm afraid they *are* going to be sad trousers, Sam,' said Ann, stirring them with a stick. 'I'm sorry, but this is the colour, and there's one good thing, it is the colour of dirt.'

'Gloomy and black as a pitchy night in winter,' said Sam.

So off he went to the woods. He picked some crimson briony berries, and scarlet rose-hips, and bright red toadstools. He brought them back and dropped them into the dye.

'Ann! Ann! Come and look,' he called, and he held up the fleece on the end of the stirring stick.

'Oh Sam! Bright red! A glorious colour,' cried Ann.

'Like a sunset,' exclaimed Tom, admiringly.

'Like a house on fire,' said Bill.

Out rushed Sam again, for blueberries and blue geranium, and borage. He dipped another wisp of sheep's wool into the juices and brought it out blue as a wood in bluebell time.

They dried the wool, and Ann fastened it to her little spinning-wheel. She spun a length of red yarn and then a length of blue. Then she knitted a new pair of trousers, in blue and red checks, bright and bold, with plenty of real pockets.

When Sam Pig walked out in his new trousers all the animals and birds came to admire him. Even the Fox stopped to stare at Sam.

'As red as my brush,' he murmured, and the Hedgehog said, 'As pretty a pair of trousers as ever I seed in all my prickly life.'

When Sam met the white mouse and her family they refused to visit his new pockets.

'We like something quieter,' whispered the mouse. 'You are too dazzling for us nowadays, Sam. Besides, we have found a lodging in an old boot. It suits us better.'

'As you will, Jemima,' shrugged Sam. He saun-
tered off to show himself to acquaintances in the
fields, to visit his old haunts in wood and lane.

Soon his trousers lost their brightness, as they
took on the hues of the woodland. They were
striped green from the beech trunks, smeared
with the juices of blackberry and spindle, parch-
ed by the brown earth herself. The sun faded
them, the rain shrunk them, and the colours
were softened by the moist air.

'I declare! There is no difference in Sam's
trousers,' Ann remarked one day. 'These might
be the old checked trousers; they are marked and
stained in just the same way. I haven't patched
them yet, but I can see a hole.'

'Yes,' said Sam, slyly, and he brought a dor-
mouse from his pocket. 'Here is a little friend
who lives with me, and he's waiting for a patch to
make his winter sleeping-quarters, Ann.'